A Shepherd's
Christmas
Story

Publishing services provided by Fitting Words—www.fittingwords.net
Cover design provided by LACreative—www.lacreative09.com

Library of Congress Cataloging-in-Publication Data

ISBN: 978-1-7331023-1-5

Printed in the United States of America

A Shepherd's Christmas Story

by

Terry Parker

Dedication

This story is dedicated to Phil and Sharon, Ronnie and Nina, Brad and Nancy, and Kip and Kim, good friends who have supported my work because they understand what a difference knowing Jesus can make in the lives of children with cancer, illnesses, or a disability.

Introduction

At the time of Jesus's birth, shepherds were considered by the Jews to have the lowest standing of all people in their community. Shepherds were always dirty because they had to clean dirt and mud off of the sheep, untangle the sheep's wool, comb out the insects that infested the sheep's skin, clean the sheep's eyes that were often clogged with a foul-smelling film, and lead the sheep through very rough fields looking for food and water. In fact, the shepherds were so dirty and smelly that they were not allowed to worship in the temple.

So why did God announce the birth of Jesus to shepherds and not to the high priest, to the leaders of the temple, or even to the important doctors, lawyers, or businessmen of the day? The Bible tells us God is most concerned about the condition of our hearts and how much we love him, not about how much money we make or how we look, so God choses those who truly want to know him and serve him as Lord and Savior.

This is a story about what might have made these shepherds God's choice for being the first to receive the most amazing news the world has ever heard.

Chapter 1

"**H**annah, I don't know what to say," ten-year-old Samuel said to his twin sister. "They are so beautiful."

Hannah and Samuel lived outside of the town of Bethlehem, in Judea, with their mother and their five older brothers, Boaz, Ezra, Amos, Ari, and Asher, who were all shepherds.

"Try them out!" she encouraged.

"You use them first and show me how they work," he said as he handed the crutches to his sister, his eyes curious and excited.

Hannah loved Samuel very much, and they had been doing almost everything together all of their lives. Samuel had been born with a twisted foot, so since they were little Hannah had been looking out for him. He could walk on this foot, but he needed the crutches to keep his balance.

Hannah didn't even notice the foot anymore when she looked at Samuel. All she saw was her kind and brave brother. But other people noticed. Hannah worked as hard as she could to make life better for Samuel.

"I've been worried, Samuel, since your crutches were beginning to hurt you so much under your arms."

"I know," said Samuel. "Mother says it is because I am getting heavier as I get older."

Hannah continued, "I have been praying and asking God to show me how I could help you. I came up with this idea, and Ezra helped me make them."

Their brother Ezra was good with his hands and could make almost anything out of wood.

"Look, Samuel, the legs are made from very sturdy olive branches. I found ones that had smaller branches at the end, and Ezra and I made them into handles. We attached a strip of leather at the top that wraps around your wrist like this," she said as she showed him how to hold the new crutches and how they would secure to his arms.

"By holding both crutches by the handles, you can support yourself using your hands and arms, and you don't have to put anything up under your arms anymore." With that, Hannah began to walk around in circles so Samuel could see just how well the new crutches worked.

"Now you try it," she said.

Samuel took the crutches from Hannah, carefully wrapped the straps around his wrists, and then took a few cautious steps forward.

"Wow! These are really great!" he yelled as he walked up and down the road.

"It might take me a little bit to get used to them, but I can already tell I'm going to like them so much more than my old ones. Thank

you so much, Hannah." He gave her a big hug and said, "Let's go show the others."

Hannah and Samuel's family had been shepherding for as long as they could remember. Their father had cared for the sheep, and his father had done the same before him. Samuel and Hannah never really knew their father very well, as he had died in a fall while he was with the sheep in the mountains when they were very little. After his death, Boaz, their oldest brother, became the leader of the family.

Samuel and Hannah took off across the field, which was rocky and steep in places. Samuel had to be very careful as he stepped over boulders and worked his way down through trees and cactus to get to where the sheep were grazing. Before long they reached the flock, and they saw their brothers around the fire cooking lunch.

"Well, look what we have here," said Ari, feigning amazement. "Someone who looks a lot like Samuel is walking around with some kind of fancy poles. Do any of you know who this can be?"

"I don't know," said Asher. "Maybe Hannah can tell us who that is."

"Brothers," said Samuel, "it's me, Samuel, and Hannah has come up with an idea for new and better crutches for me. What do you think about that?"

"Well, I'll be," said Boaz with a playful smile. "It's our own little brother, Samuel."

"They look like they work pretty good," said Ezra, and Samuel came over and gave him a big thanks for helping Hannah make them.

"Samuel," said Boaz, "I've just got one question. With those new crutches are you still going to be able to help your sister take this lamb to the inn?"

"I think so," said Samuel. "I haven't gone very far with them yet, but I seem to be getting the hang of it fairly quickly."

"Don't you worry," cried Hannah. "My brother can do anything he wants to do!"

"Okay, okay," said Boaz, "we trust you. The lamb is already in the cart. Hurry now so you can get there before dark." With that the brothers went back to eating their lunches.

As they walked toward the cart, Samuel asked Hannah, "Do you think I can pull the cart as well as I used to with these new crutches?"

"Sure you can," said Hannah, although she wasn't quite as confident as she tried to sound.

When Samuel and Hannah got to the cart, Samuel went to the front and put the harness over his head and fastened it in front of his chest so that the lines went over his shoulders and back to the cart. Hannah took her place behind the cart so she could push while Samuel pulled. This way she could also reach up and calm the lamb if it got excited or nervous.

Hannah held her breath, praying Samuel would be able to pull the cart.

"Okay, Samuel, on three. One, two, three." On the count of three Samuel pulled and Hannah pushed, and lo and behold, the cart started moving.

"It's working, it's working!" Hannah cried.

Samuel continued onward confidently. The harness and the weight of the cart gave him extra balance as he leaned forward. Hannah saw that with his new crutches, it was much easier.

The road they were taking to Bethlehem was winding and rough. Because it was not well traveled, it had not become smooth like the roads in town, so they had to be careful not to turn the cart over. As they walked, they passed olive groves and farms.

Because of his twisted foot, Samuel wasn't able to be a regular shepherd, as it was very difficult, and sometimes impossible, for him to keep up with the sheep, but this task they had been given was as important as taking care of the sheep in the field. Hannah's family provided a firstborn lamb to the high priest for festivals in the temple, and it was Hannah and Samuel's responsibility to take care of the chosen lamb and deliver it to the high priest in perfect condition.

As Hannah and Samuel made their way down the winding road and continued on the dusty path, Hannah watched Samuel closely, making sure he was walking well with his new crutches. Before long, they reached the town, and they began to see stone houses and shops where carpenters and weavers and bakers and wine makers were busy with their trades.

"How are you doing, Samuel?" asked Hannah.

"I am fine," he said, "but I'm getting awfully thirsty."

"Okay, then let's stop here and I'll go and get some water," Hannah said. She headed toward one of the water wells that had been dug long ago by their ancestors. This one was in a small square surrounded by a few shops and a manger where a few animals were being kept.

"Thank you," said Samuel as he picked out a nice spot by a nearby wall to sit and rest while he waited for Hannah.

Hannah went to the well and drew out some water and put it into the goatskin pouch that she always carried with her. When she turned around to come back, she saw three boys standing over Samuel.

Hannah knew these boys. Their leader was named Eli, and he was the town bully. And right now he was holding on to the end of one of Samuel's crutches, the other end of the crutch still fastened to Samuel's wrist. Eli had his back to Hannah.

Hannah felt panic flow through her, and her heart started pounding. She was desperate for them not to hurt Samuel or the new crutches, and she certainly did not want them to hurt the lamb or break their cart. She felt frozen and wasn't sure what to do. Then she did what she had often done in moments of fear—she prayed that God would help them.

Chapter 2

Hannah was behind the boys who were bullying Samuel. Since they all had their backs to her, they didn't notice when she put down the water and untied the sling that she always kept around her waist. Although she and Samuel were not big enough to do most of the heavy work of being shepherds, they were allowed to help guard the sheep at night against any predators. The brothers had made each one of them a sling that they could use to hurl rocks at any animal that threatened the sheep.

The hours and hours of practice out in the fields made Hannah and Samuel very accurate with their slings. She picked up two small stones from the road, then she put one in the pouch of her sling and held on to the other one. She swung the pouch around several times over her head. At just the right moment she let go of one of the two leather straps that were tied to the pouch and sent the stone flying at Eli. It hit him square on the back.

"Ouch!" Eli yelled as he turned around to see what had happened.

"What are you doing, you little brat!" he yelled at Hannah.

"I am chasing away the vermin who are bullying my brother," she spat back. "And if you don't get away from him right now I'll throw another one."

"You don't scare me," said Eli. "I don't think you could hit me a second time."

"Not only can I hit you a second time," said Hannah, "I can hit you right in your forehead, just like David hit Goliath."

Well, Hannah could see that caused Eli to think a little harder, as everyone knew the story of how David slew the giant Goliath with one smooth stone thrown from his sling.

"Even if you throw another stone, my two buddies will be on you before you can pick up a third one," he said.

"Yes," said Hannah, "but you will be on the ground. And not in any shape to see what happens next," she added.

"You don't have it in you," sneered Eli. "That last hit was a lucky shot. I bet you've never hit anything in your life!"

"How do you think those coyotes died out in the field around our sheep?" she asked. "Now get going before I lose my patience. I'm through talking." And she began to whirl the sling around over her head.

With that, Eli let go of Samuel's crutch, and he and his buddies slowly moved away, not taking their eyes off Hannah and her sling. As they went around the corner, Eli looked menacingly back at Hannah and said, "Wait till next time."

As Hannah walked back to Samuel, she thought of all the times she had stood up for Samuel. It wasn't easy growing up as the only girl with so many brothers, but she was thankful for the things she had learned. Especially for being able to use a sling. That had come in handy, and not just for protecting sheep.

When Hannah brought the water to Samuel, he said, "Wow, Hannah, that was really brave. Thank you for scaring them away."

"That's what sisters are for," she said.

"But you've never actually killed a coyote," he said. "We've only chased them away."

"I know, but I didn't say I had killed one; I just asked him a question, which made him think that I had killed one." Hannah walked over to the cart and gave the lamb a pat. "Now let's get going. We have a lot of work to do."

Hannah and Samuel were headed to an inn in Bethlehem that was owned by a prominent businessman in their community named Andar. In addition to owning the inn, he traded cloth and other goods with travelers who came through the town. He was a good friend of the high priest, and he had an arrangement with the temple to keep the firstborn lamb provided by the brothers until the high priest came to collect it.

Behind the inn, Andar had built a special manger. Only the lambs meant for the festivals were kept there. No other animals were allowed to stay in that manger, as the high priest did not want the lambs to get injured or sick. They had to be perfect, spotless, and unharmed to be acceptable to the priest.

On this particular day, Hannah and Samuel found Bethlehem more crowded than they had ever seen it. "Why are there so many people here?" asked Samuel.

"Because Caesar Augustus has ordered everyone to go to their hometown to be counted, and all these people are from Bethlehem," Hannah answered.

There were so many people with carts and animals that Samuel and Hannah found it difficult to move their little cart through the narrow street without turning it over or bumping into other larger carts. The twins decide to go down side streets in order to stay off the main road. And just when Hannah was beginning to worry that they had gotten lost, they rounded a sharp turn, and there, right in front of them was the inn.

It was an imposing building of solid stone, with several windows on either side of a massive wooden door with very large metal hinges.

Hannah went up and knocked on the door.

"Welcome, welcome," said Andar when he came to the door. "Let me look at what you have for me today. Mm-hmm," he said as he picked up the lamb and gave him a good look. "As usual, you and your brothers have sent me the very best. The high priest will be very pleased with this lamb. Now take him to the manger. Since it is late you may stay the night and I will bring you some food for your dinner. But I want you to be gone by the time the high priest arrives, Samuel. I do not want him to see that the lamb has been cared for by a crippled boy."

Hannah cringed—Andar spoke the hurtful words so casually. And why would it matter if Samuel had taken care of the lamb? That did not mean there was anything wrong with the animal.

"Come on, Hannah," said Samuel. "It's okay. I am used to it. Let us go and take the lamb to the manger."

The manger was a small enclosure built into the side of a hill behind the inn, and it was somewhat hidden from sight of any road, so very few people even knew it was there.

They opened the door to the manger, which really only a half door, and led the lamb into the shelter. It was small but adequate. On one side was a feeding trough full of fresh hay and on the other was a clay watering dish and some grain. While Samuel made them a nice bed with some of the hay, Hannah filled the dish with water and made sure there was enough grain for at least a couple of days.

Soon Hannah and Samuel settled in for the night. Hannah always slept on the floor with the lamb, who missed its mother. She would pull the lamb close to her and make it feel safe and warm.

In the quiet of the stable they began to talk about their family and God. "I love hearing Boaz teach the Scriptures to us under the moonlight and stars," said Hannah.

"Mother says that God gave Boaz a tremendous memory," said Samuel, "better than anyone in our village has ever seen."

Hannah and Samuel knew that since they weren't allowed in the temple because they were shepherds, Boaz had to think of another way to hear and learn the Scriptures. So he volunteered to clean up the temple every week. While he swept and scrubbed, he listened to the priest reading the Scriptures. The priest hardly even knew he was there. He memorized everything he heard, and then he would teach the wisdom to his brothers and sister around the fire at night.

"Mother says that she is told by her friends that Boaz knows more Scripture than even the priests," Hannah said.

As they were about to go to sleep, Samuel rolled over and faced Hannah, his hand on his head, and he said in a very serious voice, "Hannah, if I tell you something, can you keep it a secret?"

"You know we never tell anyone our secrets, Samuel," she said.

"Well, this secret is special, Hannah, and I don't even know what it means," he said.

"You can tell me anything," answered Hannah.

"I had a dream last night, right after Boaz taught us from the prophet Micah. He said that Micah prophesized that the Messiah would come from our own village of Bethlehem. I was excited about that, so I prayed that God would let you and me meet the Messiah."

"I hope he does, Samuel," she said.

"In my dream an angel appeared to me and said, 'Remember the lambs.'"

"That's all he said?" asked Hannah.

"Yes," said Samuel. "But he said it three times, 'Remember the lambs. Remember the lambs. Remember the lambs,' like he wanted to be sure I would remember. What do you think it means, Hannah?"

"I'm not sure, Samuel, but I know God will let you know eventually, and I hope that it's soon," said Hannah.

"Me too," said Samuel.

After saying their prayers, they both drifted peacefully off to sleep.

In the morning, after making certain the lamb had plenty of food and water, Hannah and Samuel started back with the cart to join their brothers in the field.

Again they found the town full of travelers.

After navigating the crowds, they finally found themselves on the main road toward their home. But as they came to a place in the road where there were low walls on either side of the road, Hannah heard some boys talking, and she could tell by their tone that they were taunting someone. She stopped and said in a soft voice, "Samuel, pull the cart over behind that wall."

Samuel did as she asked. Hannah helped Samuel out of the harness, then they crouched down and peeked over the wall. Across the road they saw a terrible sight. Eli and his two friends were striking a Samaritan boy on his head with a rod. They boy fell down and they hit him on the leg. Then they grabbed the cage he had been carrying, which contained a covey of small doves. It all happened so fast there was nothing Samuel or Hannah could do. And because they were now so far out of town, there was no one around to help.

"Okay," said Eli to his friends, "let's take these doves to the temple and sell them." He looked down at the boy and sneered, "And don't you think about following us or telling anyone what happened or we'll find you and hurt you again."

The boys walked away then, laughing at the Samaritan and talking about the money they would make selling his doves. Samuel and Hannah looked at one another, eyes wide. Samuel said, "What do we do now?"

Chapter 3

Hannah and Samuel stayed hidden behind the stone wall, wondering what to do next. "We need to help him," said Hannah. "He's bleeding, and it looks like his leg is hurt."

"I don't know," said Samuel. "The bullies might come back and attack us too."

"I don't think so," said Hannah. "You heard them. They are headed to the temple to sell his doves. Wait, here comes the high priest. Surely he will help."

They watched as the high priest and two other men with him approached the boy. One of the men said, "Look at that boy. I think he is one of those Samaritans we see bringing birds and animals to the temple to sell."

"Don't touch him," said the high priest. "He is unclean. You know we need to avoid contact with any Samaritan. Let his own kind take care of him."

Then they all just walked right on by, leaving the boy lying on the ground.

"Did you see that, Samuel?" asked Hannah. "They didn't do anything at all to help him. I don't understand that. Doesn't God teach us to help those in need?"

"You are right, Hannah. The high priest knows the Scriptures, so why wouldn't he do what God says he should do?"

"I don't know," said Hannah. "But look, I think we're in luck. Here comes one of those money changers from the temple and his wife. He must have seen this boy before, so surely he will help him."

But to their complete surprise, the wife pulled on her husband's arm and made them walk on the other side of the road from where the boy lay. As they passed where Hannah and Samuel were hidden, they said, "That boy is filthy and bloody. We don't want to get too close to him. We might catch a disease or something." And both of them hurried on by.

"Okay," Hannah said, "that settles it. We have to go help him because no one else seems to care."

"You are right, Hannah," agreed Samuel, "and if the bullies come back, I'll fight them off with my crutches."

So they came out from behind the wall, crossed the road, and knelt down beside the boy.

"Are you okay?" she asked. "My name is Hannah, and this is my brother Samuel. What's your name?"

"I think I am going to be okay," said the little boy. "My head hurts, but I've been hurt worse. I just need to rest for a while. My name is Joel. I was on my way to sell the doves I have been raising for weeks. I was going to use the money to buy food for my family. I guess that's not going to happen now."

Hannah grabbed her goatskin pouch and poured water on a cloth and washed the blood from the boy's head. Then she helped him sit up and gave him water to drink.

"That was a terrible thing those bullies did to you," said Hannah.

"Yes, and now I have to go home and tell my mother what has happened," he said, talking more to himself than to Hannah.

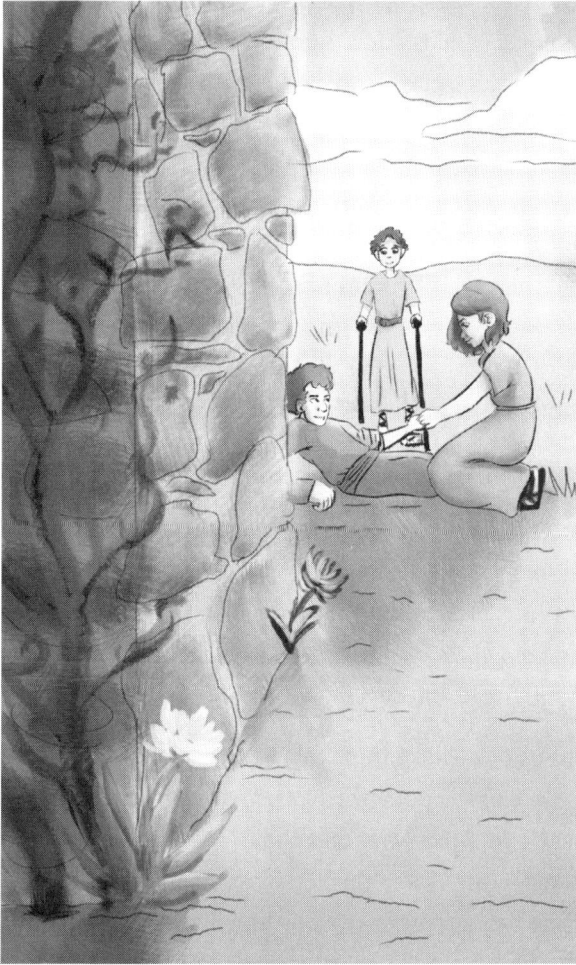

"Samuel, I think we should get off the road," said Hannah. "Just in case the bullies come back."

Hannah helped Joel up, and they went back to the wall where they had left the cart. Joel sat down with his back to the wall, and they gave him some more water.

"I've got an idea," said Hannah. "I'm going to go to the temple and see what Eli and his friends are doing. Maybe I can figure out a way to get the doves back."

"I don't know," said Samuel. "That might be dangerous. And remember, shepherds aren't allowed in the temple," he added.

"I'll be careful, Samuel. I won't let them see me. And I'm not going to go inside the temple. I'm just going to go where the money changers have all their tables set up to buy and sell the animals. Boaz says they have turned that part of the temple into a place of sacrilege and that it can't be pleasing to God. I should be able to hide pretty well with all the confusion since so many people are in town."

"Okay," said Samuel. "I'll stay here with Joel."

As Hannah hurried to the temple, she wasn't really sure what she was going to do, so she prayed that God would give her a plan. Boaz always told the twins that they should pray constantly about everything, and it certainly helped, as she asked God to build up her courage to face whatever she might find when she caught up with the bullies.

When she got to the temple, she quickly spotted Eli. There was only one place in the courtyard where doves were being bought and sold. Most of the space was taken up with people buying and selling larger animals. But as she peeked out from behind a pillar, she saw that she was too late. A merchant had already taken the doves and was handing Eli a small bag of shekels in payment for the birds.

Now what will I do? she thought. *I'll follow Eli, and maybe I'll think of something to get the money back from him.*

As Eli and the two others left the temple, Hannah followed them, staying close enough not to lose them but far enough behind so that they would not notice her. She had seen Eli put the bag of money into the pocket of his jacket, and she prayed that she could somehow get it away from him.

Just then Hannah saw three Roman soldiers coming down the road, laughing and joking with each other as they walked, and she had an idea. She leaned down and picked up a handful of stones from the road.

When the soldiers were in front of Eli and his friends, Hannah threw the rocks over the heads of the boys, and the stones landed right on the tops of the helmets of the Roman soldiers. The soldiers looked up and saw the boys, and assuming the boys had thrown the rocks, they grabbed them and demanded to know why they were throwing rocks at Roman soldiers.

The boys were squirming and fighting and twisting and trying their best to escape the grasp of the soldiers. While all that commotion was going on, Hannah, who was right behind Eli, reached into his jacket pocket, took the bag of money, and ran.

Hannah ran as fast as she could back to where she had left Samuel and Joel. She told them what had happened, and they all laughed.

When Hannah handed Joel the bag of money, he was so grateful he had to hold back tears. He tried to give Hannah and Samuel some of the money as a reward, but they wouldn't take it. They were satisfied with a promise from him that someday in the future when he saw an injured person in the road he would help that person and not just walk on by. He gave them that solemn promise and went on his way.

When Hannah and Samuel got home, they told their brothers all the exciting things that had happened to them over the last two days.

"We are all very proud of you," said Boaz, and the other brothers agreed.

Chapter 4

The next day, when Hannah and Samuel awoke, they heard their brothers talking down by the firebed. The brothers were engaged in deep conversation, with Ari and Amos waving their hands and pointing toward the desert canyons beyond the fields. The twins hurried down from their sleeping place to see what this was all about.

When they arrived, Ari was talking. "I didn't see them until they had already taken the sheep."

"Why did you leave them alone?" asked Boaz. "I've told you over and over again, we never leave the sheep without someone to watch over them."

"I can answer that, Boaz," said Amos. "After the sheep had been bedded down for the night, I began to feel very sick and told Ari I needed to go home and get some medicine from Mother."

"While he was gone," Ari said, "I noticed that the older sheep were not on the flat area above the rest of the flock where they usually sleep so I went up to investigate. While I was looking around up there, I heard some men talking loudly.

I ran down the hill to see what was going on, but I was too late. They were driving about twenty of our sheep over the rise. There were at least a dozen men, and I couldn't do anything against so many. And besides, I needed to stay and protect the sheep that were left."

"I got back about an hour later," said Amos, "and we decided to stay here and watch over the rest of the sheep until you came this morning."

"We have to go and get our sheep back," said Boaz.

"But we are so few, and they are so many, and we aren't sure where they took them," replied Amos.

"I suppose you are right," said Boaz. "So first Ezra and I will go and find the sheep and then we can all decide how we can get them back. The rest of you stay here and help guard the remaining sheep."

Ezra asked Boaz, "What will we do when we find them, and how will we know where to look?"

"I think I know where to look," said Boaz. "I bet they are stealing from others as well, and they will need a place to keep the sheep until they can sell them. There is an oasis a few miles from here that has plenty of food and water. I bet they are keeping them there."

"You are probably right," said Ezra, "but won't they attack us as soon as they see us coming?"

"I don't think so," said Boaz. "We weren't watching the sheep last night, so they won't recognize either one of us. We will pretend like we are travelers on the way into Bethlehem."

"Should we help watch over the sheep?" Hannah asked, worried about the stolen sheep and wanting to do something to help.

"Thank you, Hannah," Boaz said kindly, "but you and Samuel need to deliver the wool to the Centurion. We will find our sheep and bring them home."

While Boaz and Ezra set off in search of the sheep, Hannah and Samuel went to load up the cart so they could go back into town and deliver the lamb's wool. Even though the brothers took a large amount of wool every year to sell in the local market, the wool from the newborn lambs was special, and the wife of the Roman Centurion paid a very high price for the extra soft wool.

Hannah and Samuel took great pride in cutting, preparing, and selling the wool from their lambs to the family of the Centurion. This was an important job, not only for the money they would receive from the sale, but also because the Centurion was one of the officers in charge of Herod's army, which represented Rome in the area of Jerusalem. Everyone knew that a Centurion was the commander of as many as a hundred soldiers and was one of the most influential officials in the area.

Earlier in the week, Hannah and Samuel had cut the wool from all the young lambs. Since it was the first time these lambs had been sheared, their wool was the softest it would ever be.

To shear a lamb, Hannah would sit on the ground holding the lamb in her lap. The lambs always felt safer when Hannah held them. Then Samuel would kneel down and grab the wool in one hand and cut it carefully with the other, till the lambs all looked like they had gotten very short haircuts.

Even though they were only ten, Hannah and Samuel were experts at shearing sheep since they had been doing it since they were very young. Hannah could still remember Boaz teaching her how to calm the sheep and how he would put his strong hands over Samuel's hands as he taught him to cut the wool.

By the time Samuel had finished shearing, Hannah was always totally covered in a large pile of lamb's wool that reminded her of the snow they would sometimes see when her brothers herded the sheep through the highest hills outside of Bethlehem.

Next, they would gather the wool and pile it into the cart. Then they took the wool down to the stream, washed off all of the dirt and oil they could, and laid the wool out on rocks in the sun until it was completely dry.

The final step was to cut off any places in the wool that still were not totally clean, and then comb the wool out all in one direction so it would be ready for spinning into cloth.

On this day their cart was overflowing with beautiful white lambs' wool. They covered it with a blanket to keep any of it from falling out and to keep it clean, and off they went.

"I think this is some of the softest and prettiest wool we've ever delivered," said Hannah.

"And it's a lot more than normal," said Samuel. "Maybe we will get more money."

Once again they headed into the city. It was still crowded, but they managed to make their way through with little trouble. Soon they arrived at the Centurion's home. It was the biggest home in all of

Bethlehem. It was surrounded by a great wall, and they had to get a gatekeeper to let them in.

"I wish I could see the inside of the house," said Hannah.

"Yes, I would like to see it too," said Samuel, "but I don't think we ever will since we have to deliver the wool to the housekeeper through the back door."

When they knocked on the back door, to their great surprise it was answered by a beautiful lady they had never seen before.

"My goodness," she said, "who have we here?"

"We are the shepherds with the lamb's wool," said Hannah.

"May I see it, please?" she asked as she stepped toward the cart. Hannah noticed the woman's clean white hands and delicate jewelry.

"Please, let me take the blanket off," said Hannah. "We wouldn't want you to soil your hands. The blanket's dirty from the dusty road."

When the wool was uncovered, the lady leaned down and sunk her hands into the pile.

"This is wonderful!" she said. "I believe this is the finest lambs' wool I've ever seen. It is so white and so clean and so soft. It will make a wonderful blanket and sweaters. Thank you so much. Now come in and let me pay you."

"We've never been in the house before," said Hannah. "Do you think we are allowed?"

"Of course you are," said the lady. "It is my house."

And in they went. It was the most beautiful house they had ever seen. There were statues everywhere and wonderful stone containers with beautiful flowers and plants coming out of them. There was even a mirror on the wall, which was something neither Hannah nor Samuel had ever seen. Looking into the mirror and seeing their own reflection was amazing to them, as they had never seen themselves in a mirror before.

The floors were beautiful marble, inlaid with designs of animals and trees made from mosaic tiles of all colors. And the walls were painted in all the colors of the rainbow, and some had scenes of lakes and streams and animals grazing.

Just then a man dressed in Roman attire strode into the room. His breastplate and body armor were made of metal and shone brilliantly in the light, and he wore a scarlet robe, the color of the Romans, that flowed behind him as he walked. The children had never seen someone who looked so strong and who was so tall, but Hannah noticed that despite his daunting appearance, he had warm, kind eyes.

"Children," the lady said, "this is my husband, Marcus Aurelius Gaius. He is a Centurion in the army of Rome."

The twins were speechless until Hannah blurted out, "You are in charge of keeping the law in Bethlehem, aren't you?"

"Not only in Bethlehem, but in all the surrounding area as well," he answered.

"Then if someone steals something, you can make him give back what was stolen?" asked Hannah.

"Yes. Why do you ask?" said the Centurion.

"Because thieves have stolen some of our sheep. And if we can't get them back, we won't be able to bring you any more wool," she answered.

"Oh dear. That would be terrible," the lady said to her husband. "Their wool is the finest I've ever seen. I would hate to think that we could never get any more like it."

"I guess we need to do something about the stolen lambs, then," he said. "Wait right here for a minute," he said as he left the room.

A few minutes later he came back with another man who was also a Roman soldier.

"This is my second-in-command. He will follow you with some of my soldiers and see what can be done about these thieves."

So off they went back to the field where the brothers were watching the sheep.

When Hannah and Samuel returned to the field with the soldiers, they saw Boaz and Ezra coming back from their search.

"Well, we found the thieves," Hannah heard Boaz tell his brothers, "and sure enough, they have our sheep."

Hannah, Samuel, and the soldiers approached the group of brothers. "Oh no," said Asher to Hannah and Samuel, staring at the silent soldiers behind them. "What have you done now?"

"We've brought help," said Hannah. "The Centurion sent these soldiers to help us get our sheep back."

"Is that correct?" asked Boaz.

"Yes," said the officer who was in charge. "I am Brutus Cassius, the second-in-command of the Bethlehem garrison, and we have been ordered to help you retrieve your sheep. Now, tell me, where are the thieves? And can you identify which sheep are yours?"

"Well, we don't mark our sheep," said Boaz, "but we do know which ones are ours."

"Can I come too?" Hannah asked. She hated to leave Samuel behind, knowing he couldn't make that trek, but she wanted to be sure the sheep were okay.

"Sure," Boaz said. "Just be sure you stay out of the way, behind the soldiers. I don't want you to get hurt."

And off they went to where the thieves were holding all of the stolen sheep in the canyon. When they came over the hill and looked down into the oasis, Hannah saw a field full of sheep. There must have been at least a hundred of them.

The men who were watching the sheep looked up and saw the Roman soldiers. They talked between themselves, then a few of the men walked toward them. "What is the matter? Why are you here?"

"These brothers say you have stolen twenty of their sheep," said Brutus Cassius.

"Officer, as you can see, we have over a hundred sheep here, and we have brought them a long way. How can these men possibly prove that any of these sheep belong to them?"

"What do you say about that?" Brutus Cassius asked Boaz. "I can't just let you take twenty sheep without proof that they belong to you."

"That's very easy to do, Officer. Our sheep know us. We have raised them all since they were born, and they know my voice. Have this gentleman call to the sheep and see if any of them come to him. Then let me call to the sheep and see what happens."

"Sounds good to me," said Brutus Cassius. So he ordered the thief to call to the sheep. The thief looked worried, but he did what the officer told him to do, and he called and called to the sheep. But none of the sheep came to him.

"Okay," said Brutus Cassius to Boaz. "It's your turn."

Boaz gave the call he always gave to the sheep when he wanted to feed them or bed them down for the night. As he did, a group of sheep began to wander toward him. Then more came. Soon twenty sheep were surrounding Boaz.

"Well, it is very obvious that the sheep know their shepherd," Brutus Casius said to Boaz. "Go ahead and take the sheep back home."

Hannah was wondering what would happen to the thieves when she saw the one who had been talking to Brutus Casius take off when the officer turned to talk to Boaz and run down the path as fast as he could, the other thieves quickly following him. Brutus Casius sent some of the soldiers to capture the men, told others to stay and watch the sheep, and then he sent the rest into Bethlehem to see if other shepherds were missing any from their flocks.

Hannah and her brothers returned to their fields with their sheep, grateful they had been able bring them home.

That night, when Hannah was lying in a soft place among the rocks above where their brothers were watching the herd, her mind kept returning to the splendor of the Centurion's house. *Their home is very different from ours, but God is in both places*, she thought as she drifted off to sleep.

Chapter 5

{+I+}

A little while later, a bright light woke up Hannah. She turned to her brother lying next to her and shook him. "Samuel, wake up, wake up! Samuel, wake up! Something is happening. I'm afraid. Do you see the light?"

The light was shining all around Hannah, Samuel, and the sheep down below. It seemed to fill the entire sky and field.

"What's going on?" he asked as he sat up and held up his hands to shade his eyes.

"I don't know," said Hannah.

"Well, our brothers are all awake. They have obviously seen the light too. Look how they have gathered by the sheep. Do you think we should go down there?"

"I don't think so," said Hannah. "Let's stay here behind these rocks and see what happens."

The two of them knelt down behind the big rock and peered over the top at their brothers below and the bright light above. The field was wide and open, with only a few trees at the edge. The soft grass shone like sea water in the brilliant light. Hannah felt excited, like something wonderful was about to happen.

As they watched, a person shining as bright as any light they had ever seen suddenly appeared to be walking among the brothers. Immediately the brothers fell to the ground and covered their heads with their hands.

Hannah cried out and buried her head in Samuel's coat while Samuel put his arm around her.

"Hannah, that angel, it's the one from my dream, the one who told me to remember the lambs."

At first Hannah was still too afraid to look, but Samuel held her hand, looked into her eyes, and said, "It's okay, Hannah. You can look."

Hannah was still afraid. "Are you sure?"

Samuel replied, "I'm certain of it."

So Hannah looked down at her brothers just as the angel spoke. "Do not be afraid."

The brothers looked up and appeared to immediately become calm. They stood, but they must have still been too amazed to speak because Hannah could see that they weren't talking.

The angel continued, "I bring you good news that will bring great joy to all people."

"Samuel, what could this good news be? Why don't they ask the angel who he is and why there is such a great light?" asked Hannah.

"I think the angel is going to tell them everything they need to know," said Samuel.

And sure enough, the angel continued. "The Savior who is the Messiah, the Lord, has been born in Bethlehem, the city of David, this night. And you will recognize him by this sign. You will find him wrapped in strips of cloth and lying in a manger."

Suddenly the angel was joined by thousands of others, so many that they filled the whole sky. The light surrounding them got even brighter than it was before. And the entire army of angels began praising God and saying, "Glory to God in the highest heaven, and peace on earth to those with whom God is pleased."

Hannah was overwhelmed and grabbed Samuel's hands and began to dance around and cry out in a loud voice, "Praise God! Praise God! Praise God!"

Then, as the angels' praises filled the heavens, Hannah grabbed Samuel's crutches and said, "Come on, Samuel. We need to get down there so we can all celebrate this good news together."

They hurried as fast as Samuel's crutches could carry him down to their brothers. Ari lifted up Samuel and Amos picked up Hannah.

As she looked at all that was happening above her, Hannah thought the Centurion's house looked like the lowliest manger compared to the beauty and splendor of the sky as it filled with angels.

All at once the angels stopped singing and flew back up into heaven. Boaz exclaimed, "Isn't it marvelous, and beautiful, and exciting, and unbelievable that the angels have come to Bethlehem and announced the coming of the Messiah."

"I wonder if everyone in the city has seen what we have seen?" asked Asher.

"I don't know," said Ezra. "I'm afraid most people are still sleeping and probably have missed it."

"I don't see how anyone could sleep through that light," said Hannah. "I'm sure I will never see anything like that again. Don't you agree, Samuel?"

"I bet the scribes and priests saw it and are already telling everyone."

"Soon everyone in Bethlehem will be looking for the child. Let's go now, before the crowds grow," said Boaz.

"Okay, but we have a problem," Ezra, the practical one, said. "There must be a hundred mangers in and around Bethlehem.

Since Caesar Augustus has ordered everyone to go to the town in which they were born to be counted, Bethlehem is overrun with people right now. And they all brought their animals with them, which means that in addition to the regular mangers in the town, there are many more that have been set up to handle the crowds. It might take days to find the right one."

"What do we do, Boaz?" asked Asher. "How will we ever find the right manger?"

Just then Samuel stepped forward and said to Boaz, "I know where the child is."

"Don't be silly," said Ari. "How could you possibly know?"

"He knows because that same angel we saw tonight appeared to Samuel in a dream and told him," said Hannah.

"Don't be telling stories, Hannah," said Amos. "This is serious business."

"She isn't telling a story," said Samuel. "The angel did appear to me. But he didn't exactly tell me where to find the child. In fact, he didn't say anything about the child being born."

"See, he doesn't know anything," said Asher.

"No," said Boaz. "Let's listen to what Samuel has to say."

Since Boaz was the oldest brother and all the family knew he was in charge, they let Samuel continue without interruption.

"I had a dream the night you were teaching us from Micah, Boaz," he said. "Before I went to sleep I was thinking about the Messiah being born here in our town, and I prayed that God would allow me to meet the Messiah. In my dream an angel came to me and said, 'Samuel, remember the lambs.' He said it three times, like he wanted to be sure I didn't forget."

Samuel was growing very excited. "Now I know what he meant!"

"So tell us," said Boaz.

"You know where we take the firstborn lambs, to keep them clean and safe before they go to the temple?"

"Why, yes," said Asher. "You take them to the inn of Andar."

"That's right. And we keep that manger perfectly clean with fresh hay. I am certain that the child who has been born tonight is in the very manger where Hannah and I take the firstborn lambs."

"That's good enough for me," said Boaz. "Let's go! Amos, ask our cousins to watch our sheep and then come as quickly as you can."

"I don't think anyone needs to watch over our sheep," said Amos. "Look at them. When the bright light came around us, the sheep lay down, and they haven't moved since."

"Okay," said Boaz. "Let's just trust God to watch our sheep."

And off they went to find the manger where the Messiah had been born.

Chapter 6

As the shepherds left the field and started toward Bethlehem, Hannah was surprised to see that the town was quiet. Had no one else been awakened by the light and the angels?

"I wonder where everyone is?" asked Ari. "Why isn't the whole town out looking for the manger?"

"I don't know," said Boaz, "but up ahead is the baker's house, and I know his family is always up at this time of night baking. Let's stop and ask them if they saw the light and the angels."

They stopped at the baker's house and inquired of the family members whether they had seen a great light earlier. But they hadn't seen anything, even the ones outside who were tending the ovens.

As they walked toward Andar's inn, they stopped and asked the few others who were out at this time of night the same question, and no one had seen anything at all.

They stopped at a well to get a drink and to let Samuel rest for a moment. They knew he had walked a lot earlier in the day and had not had much rest.

"How are your crutches?" Hannah asked her brother, who had been keeping up as they walked but was now rubbing his twisted foot.

"They are wonderful, Hannah. It has just been a long day and my arms are weary."

As they rested, Hannah asked Boaz to tell them what he thought was going on and why they were apparently the only ones to see the light, the angel, and the host of heaven.

"I think this is the fulfillment of the prophecy of Isaiah," said Boaz. "Isaiah said that those walking in darkness will see a great light. We always walk in the darkness, tending the sheep at night, and now we have seen a great light. And I think the Messiah will be a great light to all the world."

"Do you really think so, Boaz?" asked Asher. "And what is the good news the angel was talking about?"

Boaz continued, "The prophet Isaiah said that a child would come, a son, and that the government would be on his shoulders. Isaiah said he would be called wonderful, marvelous, the mighty God, the Prince of peace."

Boaz looked at his siblings. "This is an amazing thing, that the angels came to us. We are not worthy to have received such good news. God has chosen us in spite of our shortcomings, in spite of our lowly position as shepherds, and we need to offer up prayers and thanksgiving for what he has done for us."

So the brothers and Hannah gathered together and knelt and praised God for all they had seen and heard.

When they were through, they continued on their way to the inn. Before they had gone very far, though, Boaz turned to Hannah and said, "Hannah, go and bring our mother so she can see the child too."

Hannah went running as fast as her legs would carry her to get her mother and bring her to see the child. She couldn't wait to tell her mother everything that had happened. Had her mother seen the light or heard the angels singing?

Just as Hannah rounded the last turn before coming to her house, two rather large and mean-looking boys stepped out in front of her. They obviously had been up to no good, as it was very early in the morning, and the only reason for them to be out was to cause trouble.

"Well, what have we here, Joshua?" one of the boys said.

"I think it is that dirty little shepherd girl, Levi," said Joshua. "What do you think she is doing out this early in the morning?"

"You leave me alone," said Hannah. "I am about some very important business."

"What do you know, her crippled brother isn't with her," Levi said.

Joshua sneered at her. "Maybe we need to make her a cripple too."

"I've got this nice rod," Levi said as he swung a stick around. "I bet I could easily break her leg with it."

"Sounds like a plan to me," said Joshua as Levi began to move toward her, slapping the rod against his hand as he walked.

"Stop right there," said a voice behind Hannah. When she turned, her heart sank. It was Eli. Now she was trapped.

"Hey, Eli. Glad you could join us," said Levi. "You can hold her while I give her a good strike on the leg."

"I'll do nothing of the sort," said Eli. "In fact, I have a rod twice the size of yours, and if you don't get out of here by the time I count to three, I'll use it on you."

"What, are you turning traitor on us?" said Levi.

"One," said Eli.

"I don't think he'll do it," said Joshua.

"Two," said Eli.

Levi and Joshua both stood there staring at Eli, clearly not sure if they should believe his threat.

"Three," yelled Eli, and he took two big steps toward the two bullies and raised his rod as if to strike. Immediately Joshua and Levi turned tail and ran.

"Wow," said Hannah, who gave a great sigh of relief. "You sure scared them. But why are you helping me?" she asked.

"Well, something happened to me yesterday," said Eli. "My mother is a widow, and she gathers gleanings from the harvest for us to eat. She had several clay jars of olive oil and several of grain, but someone stole some of our olive oil and grain. I got so mad that someone would take what they haven't worked for and would be willing to hurt other people for no good reason that I was stomping around the house and saying I would hurt the people who had taken the jars from us.

"I was so upset that I couldn't sleep, so I decided to take a walk to clear my head. Then I realized I had done the same thing to a

Samaritan boy, and I also realized I was hurting you and Samuel for no good reason, which made me a mean person. I was thinking about all of that when I heard the boys talking to you, and I came over to see what was going on."

"Well, thank you for making those boys leave me alone, but you were very wrong to steal from the Samaritan boy, and you were very mean to us," said Hannah.

"I want to make it right, Hannah, and I want to have what you and Samuel have."

"What do you mean that you want what we have?" asked Hannah.

"You probably don't know it, Hannah, but I've watched you a lot, and I've noticed that you are always quick to show kindness. I thought that was a weakness, but my mother has convinced me that sometimes it takes a really strong person to show kindness to another. And all I could think about was how weak I was, attacking you and Samuel, and how strong you were to stand up to me and my friends and protect your brother."

"I don't know what to say," said Hannah. She hesitated to believe he was truly sorry, but something in his voice made her feel sure he was being honest.

"Say that you forgive me," said Eli, "and that you'll be my friend and that maybe you and Samuel and I can be friends."

Hannah's heart filled with forgiveness and compassion for Eli. "Oh my goodness, Eli, of course I forgive you. And of course I would be glad to be your friend, and I know Samuel will as well. But right now I've got really important business to do, so I'll see you later."

And with that, she ran off.

When Hannah reached her home, she went and found her mother and told her to come quickly. As they ran back Hannah told her mother everything that had happened, and they were both filled with joy at the thought of going to see the baby who was to bring salvation to Israel—the long-awaited Messiah.

When they caught up with the others, Hannah and her mother were waiting for the brothers near the inn. Before they went to the stable, Boaz said he needed to let Andar know why all of them were there. Boaz went to the door of the inn and knocked. A loud voice from inside shouted, "There is no room at this inn. Go away!"

"Andar," called Boaz, "is that the way to greet a friend? This is Boaz, and I need to talk to you."

Andar opened the door. "I'm sorry, Boaz, my friend. People have been knocking on my door for hours, but I have had to tell them all that this inn is totally full."

Then Andar looked around, as though checking to see if anyone other than Boaz's family was around. "Boaz, I must confess something to you, and I hope you and your family will keep it a secret from the high priest."

"What is it, my friend? You can tell me, and all of us will honor our friendship."

"Well, as you know, there isn't a room for rent in all of Bethlehem, with everyone in town for the census."

"I know," said Boaz.

"Earlier tonight a young couple came to my door needing a place to lay their heads. I started to turn them away, but then

I saw the woman was about to deliver a baby, so I let them go into the manger we reserve for the firstborn lambs meant for the temple. They have a donkey, and I'm not supposed to let any other animals in there, and certainly not a woman who is about to give birth. If the priest knows I've done that, I'm in real trouble."

"Andar, you have done nothing wrong. In fact, I am so glad to be able to tell you that God has looked upon you with favor and blessed you beyond any innkeeper in the entire Roman Empire. The child born in your manger tonight is the Messiah, Andar," said Boaz.

Then Boaz told him all that had happened to them in the field that night.

Before leaving Andar, Hannah asked, "What are their names?"

"Whose names?" asked Andar, clearly surprised by the question.

"The young couple," said Hannah.

"They are called Mary and Joseph. Why do you ask?" he said.

"Well, if they are the parents of the Messiah, it seems to me their names are pretty important," she said.

Leaving Andar to go in and tell his wife the good news, the family of shepherds went to the manger and for the first time saw the child and Mary and Joseph. The child was in the manger wrapped in cloth, just as the angel had told them he would be. They were overwhelmed, and they came forward praising God and telling Mary and Joseph all of the things that had happened that night and what the host of angels had said to them.

Hannah and Samuel watched in complete silence. Finally, Samuel whispered to Hannah, "Hannah, I want to give the child a present, but I don't know what to give him."

"He is the Messiah, Samuel," Hannah said, "so you can only give him the most precious thing you own."

Samuel thought about that for a minute, and then he turned to Hannah and said, "Hannah, the most precious things I own are these crutches that you made for me. I know you saved your money to buy the leather, and you spent many hours carving the olive wood handles to fit my hands. So these crutches are as much yours as they are mine."

Hannah thought of the hours she and Ezra had spent building the crutches and the money she had saved every week to buy the materials. But she took one look at the baby Mary held in her arms and knew she would give everything she had to this holy child.

"Samuel, you can use your old ones, and though it might take a while to save the money, we will make new ones for you. Go ahead and give the child your crutches."

Hannah watched as Samuel worked his way slowly forward, and while his brothers were talking with Joseph, Samuel knelt down in front of the manger and looked up at Mary and asked, "Can I give the child my crutches as a present? They are the most valuable things I own."

Mary smiled at him and said, "Of course you can. And when he is old enough to understand, I will tell him of the young shepherd who gave him his most precious possession."

Samuel laid down his crutches beside the manger at the feet of the Messiah. When he turned around and started to walk back, Hannah cried out, "Samuel, be careful. Without your crutches, you will fall down."

Hannah started to move forward to grab Samuel and help him walk, but just then she looked up and saw Mary holding up her hand as if to tell her to stop.

Then Mary said in a quiet voice, "He won't need them anymore. God has healed him."

The whole family looked at the same time and saw that Samuel's twisted foot had become as normal as his other one. Samuel stared at his foot in amazement, and then he took a step without crutches.

Hannah jumped up and down and began to cry. "Samuel, Samuel, you can walk, you can walk!"

The brothers hugged each other in happiness for their young brother, and Samuel's mother cried tears of joy.

"Hannah," she asked, "do you remember what *Samuel* means in our language?"

Hannah replied, "Yes, Mother, Samuel means 'God has heard'!"

After all these years of praying for a miracle for Samuel, they knew God had heard their prayer.

For many years after that, they all told everyone of the things they had heard and seen and showed everyone the miracle of Samuel's healing.

Hannah never forgot that night and the wonders that were shown to the shepherds.

About the Author

Terry Parker was a longtime friend of Larry Burkett, who was heard on over a thousand radio stations with his program *Christian Financial Concepts*. After Larry's death, Terry formed the Larry Burkett Cancer Research Foundation and has written under the pen name GrandDad three other books in a series he calls the Robert P. Rabbit books. These books are primarily given away as an encouragement to children with cancer and other disabilities. Any income from the sale of this book will be used to pay for additional books to be given to Cancer Camps; Childrens Hospitals, Ronald McDonald Houses, and other places where children with illnesses are ministered to.